HOW DINOSAURS WENT EXTINCT

A Safety Guide

For museums, and the families who love them. (Including mine!)
—AD

For Steggie. The well-known, well-worn, and well-loved stegosaurus sculpture
that stands outside the Cleveland Museum of Natural History.
—JH

Dinosaur pronunciations may vary by region.
No dinosaurs were harmed in the making of this book. Probably.
Don't try anything the dinosaurs do in this book. Obviously.

ISBN 978-1-5461-2543-3

12 11 10 9 8 7 6 5 4 3 2 1   24 25 26 27 28 29

Printed in the U.S.A.   40

First Scholastic printing, January 2024

The illustrations for this book were done in Photoshop.
The book was edited by Mary-Kate Gaudet and designed by Véronique Lefèvre Sweet.
The text was set in Barthowheel Regular and Cafeteria Black, and the display type is Barthowheel Regular.
Cover design by Véronique Lefèvre Sweet

HOW DINOSAURS WENT EXTINCT

A Safety Guide

Written by **Ame Dyckman** · Illustrated by **Jennifer Harney**

SCHOLASTIC INC.

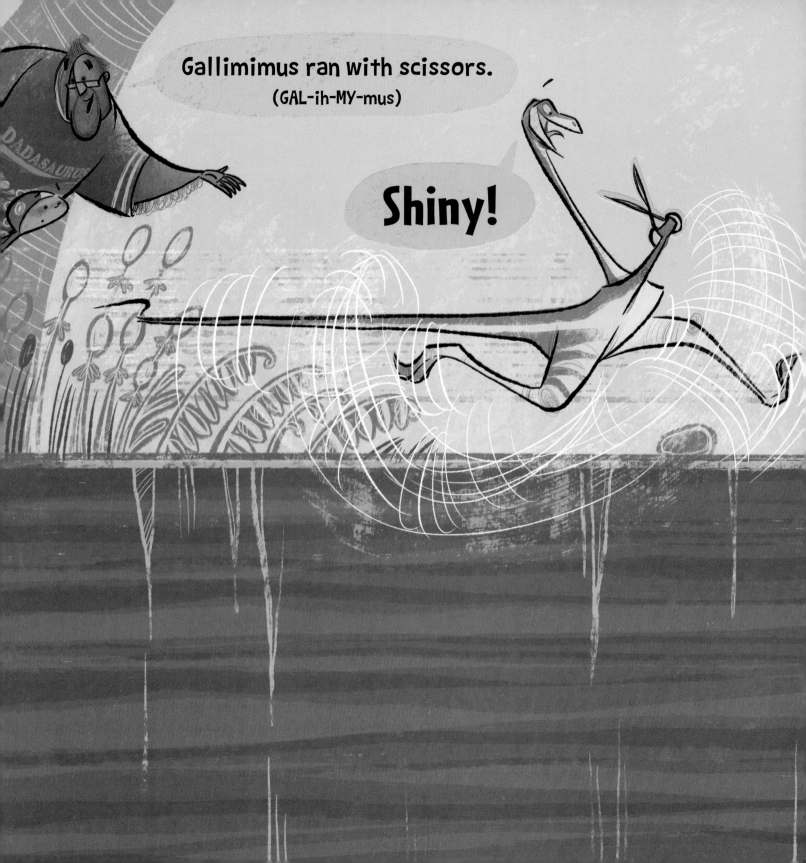

Ankylosaurus tipped in their chair.
(ANG-kuh-lo-SORE-us)

Ornithomimus jumped on the bed.
(OR-nih-thuh-MY-mus)

Pachycephalosaurus bonked stuff with their head.
(PACK-ee-SEF-ah-lo-SORE-us)

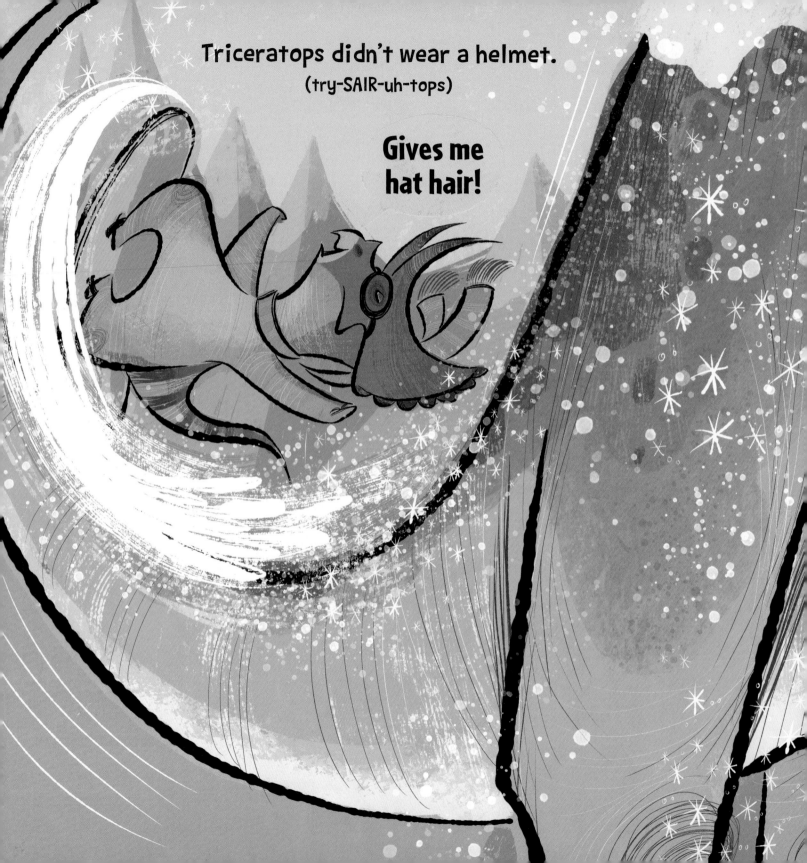

Brachiosaurus
swallowed their gum.
(BRACK-ee-uh-SORE-us)

Help!

Argentinosaurus threw a tantrum.
(ARE-jen-TEEN-oh-SORE-us)

I'm NOT tired!

Carnotaurus didn't
wash their hands.
(CAR-no-TORE-us)

Seriously?!

Compsognathus stood in shopping carts.
(COMP-sog-NAY-thus)

Gimme!

Dilophosaurus forgot to cover their coughs.
(die-LOAF-oh-SORE-us)

Velociraptor picked their nose.
(vuh-LOSS-eh-RAP-tur)

With their TOES . . .

And ate it!

Plus, Diplodocus didn't
chew their food.
(dih-PLOD-uh-kus)

Noasaurus wouldn't even
TRY to pee on road trips.
(NO-ah-SORE-us)

And all the other dinosaurs didn't clean
their rooms and got buried.

I NEVER ANY OF THINGS

AM DOING THOSE AGAIN!

Works for me.

Ame Dyckman

(*Amewritesalotasaurus*)

is not extinct. (Surprisingly, as this book is basically her autobiography. Just with dinosaurs.) Ame and her family live in New Jersey, and one of their favorite things to do together is ~~run with scissors~~ visit museums. Some of her previous books include *That's Life!*, *You Don't Want a Unicorn!*, and *Wolfie the Bunny.*

Jennifer Harney

(*Jenndrawsallthestuffocus*)

is also not extinct. Jenn lives in Cleveland(ish), Ohio, with her family, a corgi named Steve, and the ghost of the once oldest living now extinct goldfish in North America. Two of her previous books include *Underwear!* and *Swim Swim Sink.*